PLAYS FOR PERFORMANCE

A series designed for
contemporary production and study
Edited by
Nicholas Rudall and Bernard Sahlins

SOPHOCLES

Electra

In a New Translation by
Nicholas Rudall

Ivan R. Dee
CHICAGO

Library of Congress Cataloging-in-Publication Data:

Sophocles.
    [Electra. English]
    Electra / Sophocles ; in a new translation by
Nicholas Rudall.
        p.   cm. — (Plays for performance)
    ISBN 1-56663-021-5. — ISBN 1-56663-022-3 (pbk.)
    1. Electra (Greek mythology)—Drama.   I. Rudall,
Nicholas. II. Title. III. Series.
PA4414.E5R83   1993
882'.01—dc20   93-7471

INTRODUCTION
by Nicholas Rudall

Sophocles' *Electra* is one of three versions of the story of the House of Atreus that has survived. Aeschylus, in his *Libation Bearers,* told the story of Electra as a *part* of his overall vision of the issues of matricide and of human intervention in the savagery of a blood feud dictated by warring gods. In his *Oresteia* Aeschylus told this story of revenge on a cosmic scale. His human characters often seem like pawns in a divine scheme of perpetual death.

Sophocles and Euripides, in their versions of the story, chose to concentrate on the psychology of suffering. Sophocles in particular gives us his study of a creature tormented by her father's murder, her virtual slavery, her loathing of her mother, and above all her anguished powerlessness. The miracle is that this 2,500-year-old play with its distant formality speaks to us with striking psychological truth.

My translation was made with a direct eye on the stage. It is written to be spoken. It aims at clarity and simplicity. The rhythms are often short and repetitive rather than elongated and lyrical. In performance I believe this gives the distinct feeling of an elevated style—but devoid of archaisms and free from colloquialisms. As with all of the plays in this series, it is designed for performance.

The line numbers in the text refer to the Greek original.

3

CHARACTERS

PAEDAGOGUS, servant
ORESTES, son of Agamemnon and Clytemnestra,
   brother of Electra
PYLADES, friend of Orestes
ELECTRA, daughter of Agamemnon and Clytem-
   nestra
CHRYSOTHEMIS, sister of Electra
CLYTEMNESTRA, mother of Electra
AEGISTHUS, husband of Clytemnestra
CHORUS

The world premiere of this translation of *Electra*
was performed by Court Theatre on March 4,
1993. The production was directed by Mikhail
Mokeiev.

Electra

PAEDAGOGUS: Son of Agamemnon, once general at
    Troy,
Now you are here, now you can see it all,
All that you have always longed to see.
This is ancient Argos, city of your heart's pain
Where Io, tormented by the gadfly, took refuge.

And here, Orestes, is Apollo's marketplace,
The wolf-killing god.
On the left you can see Hera's famous temple.

Where we now stand, tell yourself, you can see
    Mycenae
Heavy with gold.
And the palace of the House of Atreus,
Heavy with death.   10

A time ago I took you from this place,
From the murder of your father.
Took you from your sister's arms
Who shares your blood.
I saved you then and raised you to this,
Your age of manhood,
To be the avenger of your father's murder.

Orestes and you, Pylades, dearest of his friends,
Now you must quickly plan what you will do.
The caring blackness of the night is gone.
Already the bright flame of the sun is upon us.
It stirs the morning bird's song into clearness.
Before anyone leaves this house and walks the
    streets,
Let us talk together.   20

9

We are where there is no turning back. It is time
    to act.

ORESTES: Most loved of servants, you show clearly
    The signs of your nobility toward us.
    As a thoroughbred horse, even in old age,
    Does not lose his heart and pricks up his ears,
    So it is with you. You urge me on.
    You follow among the first.

    Therefore I will make my thoughts plain.
    Listen carefully to my words.
    And where I miss the mark, guide me true.   30
    When I came to the Pythian oracle to learn
    How to take vengeance for my father
    Upon those that murdered him,
    Apollo spoke to me the words you now will hear
        from me.

    "Alone, without weapons and with no army,
    Steal the just death by treachery of hand."
    Now we have both heard the words of Apollo.
    Go then, when the time is right, into the palace.   40
    Learn all that is done there.
    Then bring us a clear report.
    They will not know you.
    You have grown old. A long time has passed.
    Your hair is flecked with white. They will not
        suspect.
    This is your story: You are a stranger,
    You have just left the house of Phanoeteus, the
        Phocian,
    The greatest of their allies. Tell them of a
        terrible accident.
    Orestes is dead. Swear it on oath.
    At the Pythian games he was tossed from his
        spinning chariot.
    Let that be your story.   50

This my father commanded: that we go first to
    his grave
And crown it with libations and thick cuttings of
    my hair. Then we shall
Come back here again,
In our hands the funeral urn ribbed in bronze,
The urn which, as you know, we hid in the
    bushes.
This is how, by stealth of speech, we shall bring
Sweet news to them that herein lies my body,
Burned and turned to ashes.
What harm is there in this if I die in word
But live in deed and win my fame?
I think no word is unlucky if it brings gain.
Many wise men I have known have been
    reported dead
But when they came home again their fame
    grew all the more.   60
And I am not afraid to say
That from this rumor of my death
I shall, like a fiery star,
Stare into the faces of my foes again.

Now, my father's land, my country's gods,
Welcome me and set me on the road to victory.
And you too, my father's house, I come to
    cleanse you,
Sent as I am in justice by the gods.   70

Do not send me from this country with no
    honor but with riches of old, restorer of my
    house.
I have now spoken.
Old friend, you must go and do what is yours to
    do.
We two will leave now. The time is right
And that is of chief importance in every act.

ELECTRA: (*within*) Oh god. Oh god. My pain.

PAEDAGOGUS: Inside the house, I heard a cry.
  Perhaps one of the servants. Orestes!

ORESTES: Her pain! Could it be Electra? Should we
  stay and listen to her tears?   80

PAEDAGOGUS: No. Apollo's will must come first.
  There is our beginning.
  Pour the libations for your father.
  Therein lies the victory and the power to act.

ELECTRA: O Holy Light
  And Air that shares the bond of earth
  When black night leaves the sky.
  How many cries of grief
  Have you heard from me?
  How many blows
  Aimed straight at the breast
  Until it was bloody?   90
  Through all the nights too
  My loathsome bed bore witness to my grief
  In this hated house,
  Grief for my father's pain.
  My father!
  The bloody god of war did not detain him
  In the savage land of Troy.
  But my mother and the man who shares her
    bed,
  Aegisthus, split his skull
  With an ax of death,
  As woodmen split a tree.
  For this no pity was given him except by me.   100
  No pity for your cruel pitiless death, my father.

  But I will never stop these cries of grief,
  These tears of sorrow,
  As long as I have eyes to see this light

Or the silver quivering of the stars.
Like the nightingale made childless by death,
I shall sing my grief for all to hear
Before these doors of my father's house.
O House of Hades and Persephone,   110
Hermes of the world beneath the Earth,
Goddess of Curses and you children of the
    gods, Holy Furies,
All you who look upon the theft of the marriage
    bed,
Come, help us, avenge my father's murder
And send my brother to me
For I am alone
And have no more strength
To bear the weight of grief that lies on me.   120

CHORUS: Child, child of a mother that brought you
    pain, Electra—
Why do you always waste your life away in
    endless grief,
Grief for the life of one long dead—
Agamemnon, killed by your mother's treachery,
Betrayed by your mother's wicked hand.
If it is not wrong to say so,
May the man who planned the murder die.

ELECTRA: Your nobility, your care means much to
    me
You are a consolation to my pain.   130
I know what you say. I know it deep within.
Nothing escapes me.
But I have no will to stop mourning my poor
    father's death.
You love me as I love you, in all ways,
So suffer this my madness,
Aaaah, let it be, I beg you.

CHORUS: You will never raise him from the streams
    of Death

13

Which comes to all,
Not with mourning...not with prayer.
If you leave sense behind,
If you pursue a grief that has no cure   140
You will destroy yourself.
In this story there is no deliverance from evil.
Why do you seek this agony?

ELECTRA: Unfeeling is the child who forgets parents
Pitilessly killed.
My heart is like the nightingale
That sings its song of grief—
"Itys," "Itys," maddened by loss,
Messenger of Zeus.
My tears are like Niobe's.   150
Niobe I call you a god
For you cry endless grief
In your grave of rock.

CHORUS: My child, this burden of grief
Does not lie upon you alone.
But your passions run higher than those within,
Those of your own blood.
Look at Chrysothemis
And Iphianassa
And that one who grows old in secret,
Mourning his life though blessed at birth,
Whom this glorious land of Mycenae
Will one day welcome home,
God willing,   160
Welcome home...as its Prince, Orestes.

ELECTRA: Orestes. I have waited for him
In my grief, wet with tears, with no rest I have
    waited.
I have no husband, no child,
I have only this endless doom of woes.
But Orestes has forgotten
What he has suffered,

14

What he has learned.
What message comes to me from him 170
That is not false?
He hungers for home. Yes. He hungers.
But he does not come.

CHORUS: Take heart, my child, take heart.
Still great is Zeus in Heaven.
He oversees all things,
He is Lord.
To him entrust your anger, excessive in its
    bitterness.
Do not be overly angry
At those you hate
Nor yet forget them.
Time is a healing god.
Orestes, son of Agamemnon, though he lingers
    away from home, 180
Will not be turned away
Nor will the God that rules the Underworld.

ELECTRA: For me, most of my life has already passed
    without hope.
I have no more strength.
I waste away, childless.
I have no husband to love and protect me.
But like an unwelcome guest
I walk the rooms of my father's house 190
Dressed in these ugly rags.
At meager tables I beg for food.

CHORUS: Your father's cry at his homecoming made
    my heart weep.
The stroke of the toothed ax of bronze
As he lay on his couch
Made my heart weep.
Treachery made the plan.
Lust did the killing.
Together they spawned a thing of terror,

15

Begetting terror,   20
Whether it was a man or a god that did this.

ELECTRA: That most hated of days
Of all the days of my life!
Oh that night!
Oh the terrible grief of that unspeakable feast.
When in shame my father saw his own death
By the hands of the two
That took my life captive,
Betrayed,
Destroyed utterly.
May the God, the Olympian, the great one   21
Send a suffering sufficient to their sins.
May they never enjoy their glory,
Murderers as they are.

CHORUS: Take care. Speak no more of this.
Don't you see that you suffer
Because of your tongue's fury?
Your destruction comes from you.
In shame you fall.
What you win is more grief,
You breed wars in your sullen soul.
You cannot fight the powerful face to face.   22

ELECTRA: Horror compelled me then,
In horror I live now.
I know it.
My fury I know well,
But in this horror
I will not hold back these
Screams of madness.
Not while life holds on to me.
What comfort is there?
What consolation?
Leave me,
Leave me, friends,
There is no cure for my grief.   23

16

Never shall I cease to mourn,
Numberless my songs of woe.

CHORUS: I speak to you in kindness
Like a loving mother.
Do not breed grief from grief.

ELECTRA: My sorrow has no natural limit.
Come, is it natural to forget the dead?
In what man is this an instinct?
I seek no honor in forgetting,
And if I ever meet some good fortune
May I never live easy,
Folding the shrill wings of lament   240
For my father's shame.
For if he that is dead
Is earth and nothing,
If he lies there neglected
And they pay nothing back,
No death for death,
Then justice, shame, and piety are dead for all
mankind.   250

CHORUS: I came to see you for your best interests
and my own.
If what I say is wrong, do your will.
We are on your side.

ELECTRA: Women, I am ashamed if I seem excessive
in my grief,
My pain.
But my life makes me do this. Forgive me.
How else could a woman of breeding behave
When she saw her father's wrongs?
And I have seen them day and night ever
blooming,   260
Never dying.
First there is my mother, the woman who gave
me life,

17

I hate her beyond all others. Then there is this:
I must live in my own house with my own
    father's killers.
They control my life. They give or take away.
So think of how my days are spent seeing,
As I do, Aegisthus on my father's throne,
Seeing him wearing my father's actual robes,
Seeing him pouring libations at the hearth
Where he killed him,
Seeing him, in the ultimate act of insult,   27
Lying in my father's bed,
His killer lying with my foul mother,
If mother I should call this woman that sleeps
    with him.
In her arrogance she couples with this curse
And fears no fury of retribution.
It is as if she mocks the murder.
She knows the day of treachery when she killed
    my father
And she marks that day with dancing,
With monthly rituals of thanks to the gods that
    saved her,
And with the cutting of the throats of lambs.   28
I see this in the house and I cry in sadness,
    waste away, mourn this
Misbegotten feast in my father's name.

I cry alone. But I cannot cry enough
To ease my heart's pain. No.
This woman, this queen in word alone, curses
    me—
"You hateful thing, loathed by the gods,
Is it only you whose father has died?
Does no other human have cause for grief?   29
May you rot in Hell! There may the gods give
    you no release
From your eternal lamentation."
That is how she humiliates me

18

Unless she hears a rumor of Orestes' return.
Then she goes insane, screams, thrusts her face
    in mine—
"This is your fault. You did this.
You took Orestes from these hands of mine.
You sent him away in secret. But you will pay for
    this. You will pay."
She howls her rage.
And there he is, her celebrated husband by her
    side,
Hissing encouragement.   300
That pillar of impotence, that utter disease.
That man who makes his battles with women.
And I, I wait for Orestes all my days,
For Orestes to put a stop to our pain.
I wait and slowly I die.
His actions are eternal tomorrows.
He kills my hopes, real and unreal.
And so, my friends, restraint is impossible,
    moderation is impossible.
I live in the midst of evil. Evil I must do.

CHORUS: Tell me, as you talk openly like this,   310
    Is Aegisthus at home or has he left?

ELECTRA: Gone. Of course. If he were home do you
    think I'd be allowed out?
No, he's in the country.

CHORUS: Then I can find the courage to talk with
    you.

ELECTRA: He's gone for now. What do you want?

CHORUS: Your brother—is he coming or just
    intending?
That is what I want to know.

ELECTRA: He says he is. But he does nothing.

CHORUS: When the task at hand is immense   32
    A man will hesitate.

ELECTRA: I did not hesitate when I saved his life.

CHORUS: Take heart. He is of noble birth.
    He will stand by his friends.

ELECTRA: I believe in him. Or how could I have lived
    so long?

CHORUS: Say no more. I see your sister
    Chrysothemis,
    Blood of your blood, daughter of your father
    and your mother.
    She has burial offerings in her hands, ritual gifts
    to the dead.

CHRYSOTHEMIS: Why have you come outside?
    What is it you want to say here?
    Will you never learn to control your empty
    anger?   33
    And yet this much I know and know it in my
    heart,
    That I am sick at what is happening.
    If I had the strength I would show them how I
    felt.
    But in this storm I must drift with lowered sails.
    I must not seem to act and then fail.
    I wish you would do as I do. And yet
    Justice is on your side, not on mine.
    But if I am to live a free life   34
    I must listen to my masters.

ELECTRA: It is strange that you, born of our father,
    his own child,
    Forget him and listen to your mother.
    When you give me advice I hear your mother's
    voice.
    Nothing is your own.

Now make a choice: be a fool or be sensible and
forget your "friends."
You said a moment ago that if you had the
strength
You would show your hatred for them.
My whole life is spent seeking vengeance for my
father,
Yet you do nothing to help. You discourage me.   350
This is cowardice heaped on shame.
Tell me—or let me tell you—what would I get if
I stopped my tears?
Do I not live?
Badly, true, but it is enough.
I hurt them and bring honor to the dead—
Perhaps down below they can feel pleasure.
But you, you *say* you hate. You say it.
But the fact is you live with your father's
murderers.
I would never give them satisfaction,   360
Not if they bribed me with those gifts you revel
in.
Set your rich table,
Live your easy life.
My inner peace is food enough for me.
As for your reputation, I reject it.
So would you, had you any sense.
At the very time when you could be known as
the daughter
Of the bravest of men,
You are known as your mother's child.
Reputation! To most people you are a coward,
A traitor to your father and your friends.

CHORUS: Enough anger! I beg you. You both have
good things to say.
You should listen to each other.   370

CHRYSOTHEMIS: Women, I am used to her and her
words. I would have kept quiet—

21

But I have heard of a terrible misfortune
  coming her way,
One which will bring an end to her mourning.

ELECTRA: Tell me of this "disaster."
  If it is any worse than my present suffering, I
  might welcome it.

CHRYSOTHEMIS: I'll tell you all I know.
  If you don't stop your public mourning they
  plan
  To send you where no light of the sun can touch
  you.
  You will live in a cave beneath the earth.
  There you can sing the sorrows of the world
  outside.
  Think about this. And do not blame me when
  you are suffering.
  Now is the time to think.

ELECTRA: So this is what they have decided to do
  with me.

CHRYSOTHEMIS: Exactly. As soon as Aegisthus
  returns.

ELECTRA: As far as I am concerned, that can't be
  soon enough.

CHRYSOTHEMIS: Why do you pray for that, my poor
  sister?

ELECTRA: Let him come if he will do as you say.

CHRYSOTHEMIS: What do you want? Are you out of
  your mind?

ELECTRA: I want to be as far away as possible from
  all of you.

CHRYSOTHEMIS: Don't you care for your life?

ELECTRA: My life is beautiful,
The envy of the world.

CHRYSOTHEMIS: It would be, if you learned to be sensible.

ELECTRA: By being a traitor to those I love? Is that your advice?

CHRYSOTHEMIS: No, it is not. But to yield to those who have power.

ELECTRA: Yes. Kiss their feet. That's not my way.

CHRYSOTHEMIS: But to die from stupidity! Where's the good in that?

ELECTRA: I shall die, if die I must, revenging my father.

CHRYSOTHEMIS: My father will forgive me. I know that. 400

ELECTRA: These are words that only a coward would admire.

CHRYSOTHEMIS: You resist me to the end. You will not listen then?

ELECTRA: Never. God keep me from such emptiness of mind.

CHRYSOTHEMIS: Then I must go and do what I was told.

ELECTRA: Where are you going?
Those burnt offerings—who are they for?

CHRYSOTHEMIS: My mother told me to place them on father's tomb.

ELECTRA: What are you saying? The man she hated above all others?

CHRYSOTHEMIS: Whom she murdered. That is what you meant to say.

ELECTRA: Which of her friends persuaded her? Whose idea was this?

CHRYSOTHEMIS: I think it was a terrifying dream she had.

ELECTRA: Gods of my father, be with us now.   410

CHRYSOTHEMIS: Why should a nightmare make you so confident?

ELECTRA: Tell me the dream and I'll tell you why.

CHRYSOTHEMIS: I cannot tell you much. I know very little.

ELECTRA: Tell me all the same.
It is the little things that make us or break us.

CHRYSOTHEMIS: The word is that she saw my father
Your father and mine.
He came to life again,
To live with her again.
He took the scepter,
Which once was his,
Which now Aegisthus bears,
And planted it in the hearth.   420
From it foliage sprang,
Luxuriant leaves that cast their shadow over all
   this land,
This Mycenae.
This I heard from someone who was there
When she told her dream to the light of the
   Sun.
This is all I know.
No more.
Only that she sends me because of her fear.
I beg you, by the Gods of this our land,

Listen to me and do not die because of your
stupidity.
If you reject me, she will come after you and
punish you.   430

ELECTRA: My sweet sister. Nothing must touch his
tomb.
Nothing of what you are carrying.
It would be wrong, sacrilege even,
For you to place upon our father's grave
Sacrifices and offerings from a woman that is
our enemy.
Throw them to the winds
Or hide them in a deep hollow of the earth,
Somewhere where not a trace of them
Could touch my father's bed of death.
Keep them for *her*,
Treasures beneath the earth when death takes
her.
Listen. If she were not the most arrogant of all
women,
She would not attempt to pour these loathsome
libations   440
On the body of the man she murdered.
Think. Can you imagine that his corpse, deep in
his grave,
Would accept offerings from her,
The woman who killed him, robbed him of his
honor?
The woman that cut off his hands to stuff in his
armpits,
The woman that washed the stain of her hands
In the blood of his head.
Look. These offerings will not wash her clean of
murder.
Never. Set them aside.
Cut a lock of your own hair

25

And one from mine, his pain-ravaged daughter.
A small offering, but all I have.   45
Give it him, this lock of shining living hair
And this my plain waistband.

Kneel at his grave.
Pray that from the earth he will arise to help us,
A friend against his enemies.
Pray that his son Orestes may live,
Set his foot upon his enemies,
And gain the upper hand.
Then may we in future time dress his grave
With richer hands than now.
I believe, oh yes, I believe that it was he
That thought to send this ill-omened dream
    upon her.   46

But upon you, my sister, falls this present task.
On you it falls to be my help and his,
That man loved most of all,
Your father and mine,
That man beneath the earth.

CHORUS: The girl speaks wisely.
    If you are sensible, my child, you will follow her
        advice.

CHRYSOTHEMIS: I will. It is unreasonable for us
    To quarrel over what is just.
    But now we must hurry.
    But if I do this, my friends,
    I need your silence.
    If my mother gets word of this,   47
    I know that I shall suffer much for my actions.

CHORUS: If I am not bewildered,
    If I am a prophet
    In touch with sound judgment
    Then Justice will come.

Justice, herself a prophet, will come
With a just victory in her hands.
She will come after them, my child.
And it will not be long.
Confidence entered into me
When I heard
Of this dream that breathes sweetness.   480
The King of the Greeks, your father,
Has never forgotten.
The ax has not forgotten,
The ax that long ago
With double tooth of bronze
Cut him down
In shame and squalor.

And the Fury will come,
She will come,
Many her hands,   490
Many her feet,
Feet of bronze,
Hidden in an ambush of terror.

They fought for a forbidden bed,
For a forbidden marriage
Stained with murder.
They sinned.

And so
Confidence entered into me
That never, never
Would such an omen come upon us
Without fear
For those that did the crime,
Did it together.

In truth
There is no prophecy for mortal men
In dreams of terror
Or in the word of the Gods

If this vision of the night   50
Is not fulfilled.

We live an ancient curse,
The curse of Pelops,
The chariot race that brought
Grief upon grief,
Death upon death.
Since Myrtilos found his bed of death in the sea,   51
Hurled from his golden carriage,
Hurled to his Destruction.
For never a moment since
Has destruction left this house.
Grief upon Grief.

CLYTEMNESTRA: They've let you out, I see,
     wandering about.
  That's because Aegisthus isn't here.
  He always keeps an eye on you.
  Keeps you from going amongst the people,
     disgracing your family.
  But now that he's away you pay no attention to
     me.
  Although you've told the world at length   52
  How cruel I am, how unjust, how domineering,
  How I insult you and your friends.
  Arrogant I am not.
  But if you abuse me all the time
  I will abuse you in return.
  Your father, yes. Always your father.
  That's your only excuse—that he was killed by
     me.
  By me. Yes. I know it well. I do not deny it.
  But I was not alone. Justice was my partner.
  Justice took his life. And you would have
  Served Justice if you had your head on straight.
  This father of yours—for whom you live in
     grief—

28

Alone of all the Greeks was the cruel one.   530
He sacrificed your sister to the Gods.
He had not worked hard for her as I had.
He did not give birth to her as I did.
He spawned her only.
Tell me why he sacrificed her? Why?
Was it to save the Greeks?
My daughter was not theirs to kill.
Was it to save Menelaos, his brother?
Is that why he killed my child?
Then should he not have paid for his crime?
For Menelaos had two children.
Should they not have died instead of mine?
It was for their parents' honor   540
That all the Greeks set sail for Troy.
Perhaps the God of Death longed to feast
Upon my children rather than theirs?
Perhaps this "father"—my curse upon him—
Perhaps this father had lost his love of my
     children
And felt it only for those of Menelaos?
This was the act of a father who had no
     thoughts,
Or if he had they were evil thoughts.
That is how I see it. I care not if you disagree.
The dead girl, if she could speak,
Would take my part.
But I do not despair at what has happened.
If you think me wicked,
Keep your self-righteous thoughts to yourself   550
And blame the world.

ELECTRA: This time you abused me first.
     You cannot say you were provoked.
     I said nothing to hurt you.
     But I would like, if you will allow it,
     To speak on behalf of my dead father and sister.

29

CLYTEMNESTRA: Of course. You have my permission
    to speak.
  If you had always spoken as you just did
  You would not have been so painful to listen to.

ELECTRA: Then I will tell you what I think.
  You say you killed my father.
  What could be more shameful
  Than to admit that?   5(
  —With justice or without.
  But I will argue that it was
  Without justice that you killed him.
  You were seduced into murder
  By that evil man with whom you now live.
  Ask Artemis, Goddess of the Hunt,
  Why she held all the winds in stillness at Aulis.
  No. *I* will tell you why.
  You do not have the right to speak to her.
  This is the story I have heard:
  My father was hunting and while in her sacred
    grove
  He startled from beneath his feet
  A horned and dappled stag.
  He loosed his arrow, hit the stag,
  And then uttered some casual boast.
  Artemis was angry at this   5`
  And therefore stayed the Greeks.
  It was her intent that my father
  Sacrifice his daughter
  In return for the slaughter of her sacred beast.
  That is why my sister was sacrificed.
  Otherwise the army could not move
  Either homeward or to Troy.
  He resisted hard, fought hard against it.
  In the end he had to sacrifice her.
  And it was not for Menelaos
  But even if—I'll take your side now—

Even if he did this for his brother—
Is that a reason for you to murder him?
By what law?   580
If this is the law you lay down for men,
Take care that you are not laying down
Ruin and regret for yourself.
For if we kill one for another,
You would be the first to die
If you met with true justice.
Take a close look at yourself.
See if you are merely offering an excuse.
Tell me why, if you could,
Why you are committing an act beyond shame—
Sleeping with the murderer with whom you
    killed my father.
And you are making children with him.
But you drive out your own legitimate children,
Children born of a legitimate marriage.   590
What am I supposed to praise in this?
Will you argue that this too is done
To pay for your daughter's death?
Even if you say it,
It is still an act beyond shame.
There is nothing good in marrying an enemy
For the sake of a daughter.
But I do not even have the right to criticize you.
All you can say—and it is all you say—
Is that I am abusing my mother.
I do not think of you as my mother.
No. You are my personal tyrant.
My life weighs heavy on me.
I live in a world of suffering   600
Inflicted by you and your bedmate.
But remember—your other child is not here—
Though he barely escaped the violence of your
    hand.
My sad Orestes lives out a life of painful exile.

How often have you accused me
Of saving him to be your murderer.
If I had the power that is what I would have
done.
Know that.
And for that reason you can proclaim to the
world
That I am a traitor, an abuser, a creature with
no shame.
But if these are the skills I was born with,
It is merely a reflection on the woman who gave
me birth.

CHORUS: I see her anger.   61
But whether she speaks in justice
That I can no longer see.
I know not what to think.

CLYTEMNESTRA: *I* do not have to think of her at all.
Look how she vilifies me, her own mother.
She shows no respect.
No. Her arrogance knows no limits.
She knows no shame.

ELECTRA: Not true.
I am ashamed, even if you do not believe me.
I know why I behave so strangely,
So unlike myself.
You hate me.
That, and the things that you do to me,
Force me to behave this way.   62
My shameful actions I learned from yours.

CLYTEMNESTRA: Impudent creature!
I and my words, my actions
Give you too much freedom to talk.

ELECTRA: You do the talking, not I.
You do the deeds
And the deeds produce the words.

CLYTEMNESTRA: By Artemis, your arrogance will be
   punished
When Aegisthus comes home.

ELECTRA: You see?
   You give me permission to speak,
   And then you fly into a fury.
   You do not know how to listen.

CLYTEMNESTRA: At least give me some peace.   630
   Let me sacrifice in silence
   Since I have permitted you to say all you
      wanted.

ELECTRA: I allow you.
   In fact I urge you to sacrifice.
   You cannot blame my lips.
   They will speak no more.

CLYTEMNESTRA: You there! Raise the offerings on
   high, the earth's fruits.
   I pray to the God that I may be freed from my
      fears.
   Apollo, Protector, hear me, hear my whispered
      cry.
   For I am not among friends, nor,
   While this girl stands beside me,
   Can I tell all to the light of your day.   640
   She would sow the seeds of slander
   To the whole city in her envy,
   In her unending scream of lies.
   Hear me then. This is my prayer.
   The dreams of double meaning I have seen this
      night.
   Lord Apollo, make what is good in them turn
      out well.
   Turn what is evil upon those who do us evil.
   If there are some who plot and scheme

33

To deprive me of my present wealth, protect
  me.
Let me live this my life free from harm.
Let me be mistress of the house of Atreus   6₅
And its Queen.
Let me live with those I love as I do now,
Enjoying the goodness of my days
With the children who do not hate me,
Do not cause me pain.
O Lord Apollo, this is my prayer.
Hear it in kindness.
Grant to all of us what we ask.
I cannot speak all that I would say
But you are a god and know it,
Know it well.
The children of Zeus see everything.

PAEDAGOGUS: Ladies, strangers of course to me,   6₆
  Is this the palace of King Aegisthus?
  I need to know for certain.

CHORUS: Yes sir, this is the palace.
  You were not wrong.

PAEDAGOGUS: Would I be right in thinking that this
    lady is his wife?
  She has the looks of a queen.

CHORUS: Again you are right. She comes.

PAEDAGOGUS: Greetings, your majesty.
  I bring news from a friend.
  Pleasant news for you and Aegisthus.

CLYTEMNESTRA: What you have said, I welcome.
  First tell me, if you will, who sent you.

PAEDAGOGUS: Phanoeteus, the Phocian.   6₇
  And what he charged me to tell you is grave.

CLYTEMNESTRA: What is it, sir? Tell me.
  He is a friend.
  There must be friendship in his words.

PAEDAGOGUS: Orestes is dead.
In one brief word I tell all.

ELECTRA: Aaah, my pain.
This is the day of my death.

CLYTEMNESTRA: What did you say?
What did you—don't listen to her.

PAEDAGOGUS: Orestes is dead.
I said it then.
I say it now.

ELECTRA: Grief kills me.
I am no more.

CLYTEMNESTRA: (to Electra) Leave us alone.
How did he die?
I want the truth.

PAEDAGOGUS: This is why I was sent.   680
I will tell you all.
He had gone to the Delphic games,
The most glorious games in all of Greece.
He heard the herald announce the first
   contest, a foot race.
As he entered the stadium he seemed to radiate
   light.
All gazed at him in wonder. He ran as well as he
   looked.
He won the race and he left the track bathed in
   glory.
I could say much but I must be brief.
Never have I seen a man of such strength, such
   power.
Know this one thing:
In all the contests announced by the stewards
He was victorious.
The people roared their approval as he was
   given the prize.   690

35

"Orestes, from the city of Argos,
Son of Agamemnon who once gathered
The glorious army of Greece."
So it was.
But when a God means harm, there is no
     escape.
Even for a strong man.
The next day at the setting of the sun
There was a chariot race.
Orestes entered.
There were many other contestants.
One from Achaea, one from Sparta,
Two men from Libya, both expert charioteers.
Orestes was the fifth.
He manned a chariot pulled by Thessalian
     mares.
The sixth was from Aetolia.
His horses were young and golden.
The seventh from Magnesia.
The eighth from Aenia with a team of white
     horses.
The ninth from Athens, city of the Gods.
And then a Boeotian. Ten chariots in all.
The stewards placed them in their allotted
     positions.
They stood at the ready. The trumpet sounded.
And they were off.
The drivers shouted at their horses, urging
     them on.
They slapped the reins.
The stadium shook with the clash and clatter of
     chariots.
Dust rose in a cloud.
They were a hurtling, seething mass.
Each man lashed his whip,
Each man trying to put his axle
Or the snorting mouths of his horses

Past the others.
The backs of the horses, the very wheels of the
    chariots
Were lathered in foam. Those behind breathed
Horse breath in pursuit.
Thus far all the chariots were unscathed.
Then the hard-mouthed colts of the Aenean
Bolted and at the end of the sixth lap
Careened into the Barcaean chariot. Head on.
Then, from this one accident, one crashed
Into another, chariot piled upon chariot
Until the whole course was a sea
Of wreckage. But the Athenian, a skilled
Charioteer, saw what was happening,
Checked his team, and passed by the seething
Mass of horses in the middle.
Orestes had been in the back of the field,
Holding his horses back, trusting in the finish.
Now when he saw that only the Athenian
Was left he gave a great shout that pierced
His horses' ears and set off in pursuit.
He drew level, axle to axle.
Now one, now the other would get
His horse's head in front.
Orestes always drove tight at the corners.
Just grazing the post with his wheel
He gave rein to the horse on the right,
The trace horse, and checked the one on the
    left.
In all the other laps Orestes—oh the pity of it—
Had been safe. His horses were safe.
But this time he let go of the left rein
As the horse was turning the corner.
He struck the pillar. He did not see it.
His axle broke in the middle.
And he was hurled from the chariot
And became entangled in the reins.

As he fell to the ground his horses bolted
To the middle of the course. A cry of grief   75
For the young man filled the air when the
    crowd
Saw him fall. They mourned his courage,
Mourned his sad end. At times he was
Dashed to the ground, at times tossed into the
    air.
Finally the grooms, barely able to stop
The runaway horses, cut him loose.
He was so covered in blood that his friends
Could not recognize his wretched corpse.
They burned him on a funeral pyre
And his ashes, poor remnants of a mighty
    frame,
Were placed in an urn. Some Phocians,
Selected to do it, have brought him home   76
To be buried in his father's country.
That is my story, painful in the telling,
But for those of us who saw it
The greatest disaster these eyes have ever seen.

CHORUS: (*moans*) Aah. Aah. The ancient family of
    Kings
    Is gone.
    Perished, perhaps, root and branch.

CLYTEMNESTRA: Zeus, what should I say? Should I
    count my blessings?
    Or say, "Terrible—but for the best."
    Indeed I live a sorry life if I must
    Save that life by my own misfortune.

PAEDAGOGUS: Why, my lady, does my story make
    you thus dejected?

CLYTEMNESTRA: To give birth is a strange thing.   77
    A mother cannot hate the child of her womb
    Even when it brings her harm.

PAEDAGOGUS: Our journey then, it seems, was
     without purpose.

CLYTEMNESTRA: Not without purpose. How can you
     say that
   If you have brought certain proof of death?
   Yes, he got breath from the breath of my soul,
   But he tore himself from my breast,
   From my loving care. He became an exile
   And a stranger. When he left this land
   He never looked into my eyes again. No.
   He accused me of his father's murder.
   Threatened me with terror.
   Neither by night or day could sweet sleep   780
   Cover my eyes. No. Time hovered over me,
   Leading me step by step to inevitable death.
   But now, this one day has freed me from fear
   Of him and of her. She was the greater curse.
   She lived with me, always sucking my lifeblood
     dry
   As though it were wine. Now perhaps I shall
     find peace
   From her threats. I shall live again in the
     daylight.

ELECTRA: Oh God! My Pain! Orestes. Now I must
   Mourn your death indeed when even in death
   Your mother heaps insults upon you. Is this
     right?   790

CLYTEMNESTRA: Not yet for you. But he's right as he
   is.

ELECTRA: Nemesis, hear how she speaks of the
   newly dead.

CLYTEMNESTRA: She has listened before. As was
     right.
   And she did
   What was right.

39

ELECTRA: Pride! Arrogance! Yes. Now fortune is on
your side.

CLYTEMNESTRA: Will you not stop this? You and
Orestes—

ELECTRA: Orestes. Yes, we are stopped. We cannot
make you stop.

CLYTEMNESTRA: Sir, your journey will be worth your
while
If you have stopped her interminable noise.

PAEDAGOGUS: Well, I should go now if all is done
here.

CLYTEMNESTRA: Certainly not. That would be
ungrateful of me   80
And unworthy of the friend who sent you.
No, come inside. Leave her out here
To shriek her pain for those she loves.

ELECTRA: There's a grieving mother. See how she
wept,
The agony of her bitter tears,
The grief of a mother for a dead son.
She left us with laughter in her eyes.
Oh God.
Sweet sweet Orestes, your death is my death.
You have torn from my heart the only hope   810
I had left, that you would live
And some day come back to avenge
My father and me and my pitiful life.
Now where am I to turn? I am alone.
I have lost you. I have lost my father.
Again I am a slave amongst those I hate most,
My father's killers. Is my life not beautiful?
But I will not enter the house again. Never.
To live with them? Never. I will stay here at the
gate,

40

Unloved, I will starve my life away.
If they object, those two inside, they can kill me.
Death would be a blessing. My life is a curse.   820
I do not long for life.

CHORUS: Where are the thunderbolts of Zeus?
Where is the burning sun?
If they see this
And hide this
And are silent?

ELECTRA: (*a mournful cry*) Aaai. Aaai.

CHORUS: My child, do not weep.

ELECTRA: (*again*) Aaah.   830

CHORUS: Do not cry too loud.

ELECTRA: You will destroy me.

CHORUS: How?

ELECTRA: If you offer me hope,
When all is clear,
When they are gone,
Gone to the House of Death.
And as I waste my life away
You beat me further down.

CHORUS: Remember King Amphiaraus.
He was caught in a woman's
Golden snares.
And now beneath the earth—

ELECTRA: Aaaa.   840

CHORUS: He is King of every soul.

ELECTRA: Aiai.

CHORUS: Yes. Remember. The murderer—

ELECTRA: Was killed.

CHORUS: Yes.

ELECTRA: I remember. For him amidst the pain
  There came an avenger.
  But for me there is none.
  Once there was but he is gone,
  Torn from my arms by Death.

CHORUS: Yes, grieve. You own grief.

ELECTRA: I am my own witness, beyond a witness,   85(
  To this,
  This life lived month
  After month
  In agonies hurled at me
  From all sides.
  Eternal agonies.
  Endless agonies.

CHORUS: We know why you weep.

ELECTRA: So do not, do not lead me where—

CHORUS: What do you mean?

ELECTRA: Where there is no hope, no help,
  None of my blood by my side.

CHORUS: Death comes to us all.   86(

ELECTRA: Yes, but to die as he died,
  Sweet brother,
  Tangled in the dust,
  Bloodied by the hooves
  Trampling him in terror.

CHORUS: Death is a sudden thief.

ELECTRA: Yes. And now he is gone, buried.

CHORUS: Aaa.

ELECTRA: By hands that were not mine,   87(
  With tears that were not mine.

42

CHRYSOTHEMIS: I am filled with joy, sweet sister,
I have run here in haste
Not caring what people thought.
I bring you happiness and release
From all your troubles, all your griefs.

ELECTRA: Where could you find relief for my pain?
There is no cure.

CHRYSOTHEMIS: Orestes has come home. Hear it.
Know it.
In the light of day you can see him as you see
me.

ELECTRA: Have you lost your mind from grief?
Or do you mock my troubles and your own?   880

CHRYSOTHEMIS: I swear by my father's house I do
not mock.
I say the truth—he is home and with us.

ELECTRA: Oh you fool! Who told you this?
Who has tricked you into believing this?

CHRYSOTHEMIS: I believe it because I have seen
The living proof with my own eyes.

ELECTRA: What proof? What have you seen, you
poor thing?
What makes your heart burn with this
unquenchable fire?

CHRYSOTHEMIS: Listen, I beg you, listen to me.
Then call me either wise or a fool.   890

ELECTRA: Tell me then if it brings you pleasure.

CHRYSOTHEMIS: I shall tell you all that I saw.
When I went to father's ancient grave,
Immediately I saw streams of freshly poured
milk
Flowing from the top of the mound.

43

The grave itself was covered with a wreath
Of all kinds of flowers. I saw this and was
  amazed.
I looked around to see if there was anyone
  nearby.
There was not a sound. I approached the grave.
I saw there on top of the tomb a lock of hair.
Something jumped inside me. I recognized it.   900
I know that I was looking at an offering
Left by Orestes whom I love so deeply.
I took it in my hands, not breathing a word.
I did not want to risk saying anything
That would bring bad luck. But in my joy
My eyes filled with tears. I knew it then.
I know it now: this offering could only be from
  him.
Who else, other than you or I, would care to do
  this?
I did not do it. That I know. Nor did you.   910
You couldn't. They do not let you leave the
  house
Even to pray. Our mother would not do it.
That is not something she likes to do.
Certainly not in private.
These are ritual offerings from Orestes.
So, my sweet one, take heart. It is not always the
  same
God that hovers over the same people.
In the past the God hated us. But now perhaps
This day will see the beginning of much good.

ELECTRA: As you spoke I felt sorry for you, you poor
  fool.   920

CHRYSOTHEMIS: Why do you say that? Didn't my
  words bring you joy?

ELECTRA: You do not know where you are or where
  your
  Thoughts are taking you.

44

CHRYSOTHEMIS: I know what I saw. It was there
before my eyes.

ELECTRA: My dear sister, he is dead. Your safety
died with him.
Look to him no more.

CHRYSOTHEMIS: My God! Who told you this?

ELECTRA: Someone who was there when he died.

CHRYSOTHEMIS: Where is he? I don't know what to
think.

ELECTRA: He is in the house. An honored guest.
A welcome guest.

CHRYSOTHEMIS: My God! Then who on earth could
have placed   930
So many offerings on father's grave?

ELECTRA: Perhaps someone put them there in
memory
Of Orestes now that he is dead.

CHRYSOTHEMIS: I am cursed. I ran here to tell you. I
was so happy.
Little did I know where our bleak fate had
brought us.
But now that I am here I find old griefs
And new griefs.

ELECTRA: Perhaps that is how you see it. But listen
to me
And you can lift the weight of suffering that lies
upon us.

CHRYSOTHEMIS: How can I bring the dead back to
life?   940

ELECTRA: I am not a fool. That is not what I mean.

CHRYSOTHEMIS: What do you want me to do—if I
can do it?

45

ELECTRA: Be brave and do what I tell you.

CHRYSOTHEMIS: If I can help I will not say no.

ELECTRA: Look, success means a struggle.

CHRYSOTHEMIS: I understand. I will help to the best
of my ability.

ELECTRA: Listen then to the plans I have made.
You know as well as I that we have no friends
To help us. None. Death has taken them. 95
They are gone. We two are all that is left.
As long as I knew that my brother was alive and
well
I held on to the hope that he would come some
day
To avenge the murder of his father. Now he is
no more.
I turn to you. You must help me, sister of your
own blood.
You must help me kill our father's murderer,
The man who struck him down—Aegisthus.
I have nothing to hide from you.
What are you waiting for? You say nothing?
Why?
What hope do you have left that still exists?
Grieve now for the loss of our father's wealth, 96
Mourn now for the years lost, no marriage, no
husband.
Do not hope to get them now. Aegisthus is no
fool.
He will not allow your or my children to live.
They would clearly be a threat to him.
But if you follow the plans that I have made
You will earn the respect for your devotion
From the dead below, father and brother.
That first, then as you were born a free woman
You will be called free for the rest of your life. 97

46

And you will find a husband worthy of you.
All men love the strong, the noble of spirit.
Don't you see the reputation, the glory you will win
For yourself and for me if you do this?
Citizen and foreigner alike will look on us
And receive us into their hearts with praise:
"Look upon these two sisters," they will say.
"They have restored their father's house,
They risked their lives, stood fast against murder
Even in the face of enemies at the height of their power.   980
They deserve our love, deserve our respect.
In our religious and public festivals we must
Honor these women for their men's hearts."
That is what everyone will say of us,
And in life and in death, glory will be ours.
My dear sister, join me in the fight.
Let us struggle together for father and brother.
Free me from my pain. Free yourself, knowing in your heart
That for the nobly born to live in shame
Is the depth of shame.

CHORUS: In times like these caution is a friend   990
To those who speak and those who listen.

CHRYSOTHEMIS: Even before she spoke, my friends,
She should have sought prudence if she had good sense.
She has not. It is rash, foolish, arrogant
To arm yourself and call on me to help.
Don't you see? You are a woman, not a man.
You are not a match in strength for your enemies.
Their god protects them, prospers day by day.
Ours falters and comes to nothing.   1,000

47

Who could take arms against a man of
　　Aegisthus' power
And emerge untouched, free of destruction?
Look, we are suffering now and we will suffer
　　more
If anyone hears of your plans. Where is the
　　freedom,
Where the victory and glory if we die in shame?
Not that I fear death. No. What I fear most is
To want to die and not to have that death.
I beg of you, before you destroy us all,
Before you wipe our race from the face of the
　　earth,
Hold your anger in check. You can be sure
That all you have said will remain a secret.　　　　　1,
Nothing will be done. Curb your will. You are
　　weak.
Learn to give in to those who have power.

CHORUS: Listen to her. The best human gifts are
　　caution
And wisdom.

ELECTRA: You said what I expected. I knew you
　　would reject
What I proposed. I have to act alone.
The deed must be done by my own hand.
And done it shall be.

CHRYSOTHEMIS: Ahhh.　　　　　　　　　　　　　　1,
I wish you had felt like this when father was
　　killed.
Then you would have done all that had to be
　　done.

ELECTRA: My nature was the same. My judgment
　　weaker.

CHRYSOTHEMIS: Find that judgment now. Keep it till
　　you die.

48

ELECTRA: When you say that, I know you will not help me.

CHRYSOTHEMIS: To make the attempt at all would only court disaster.

ELECTRA: I envy your good sense, hate your cowardice.

CHRYSOTHEMIS: If ever you praise me, I shall be as calm as I am now.

ELECTRA: Praise! Never from these lips.

CHRYSOTHEMIS: Let time be the judge.   1,030

ELECTRA: Leave me. You cannot help me.

CHRYSOTHEMIS: I can help. But you will not listen.

ELECTRA: Go. Tell everything to your mother.

CHRYSOTHEMIS: I do not hate you. I could not do that.

ELECTRA: Don't you see how you dishonor me?

CHRYSOTHEMIS: No dishonor, only concern.

ELECTRA: You expect me to follow your idea of justice?

CHRYSOTHEMIS: Think and you will see that we share the same idea.

ELECTRA: You sound so sensible. But you are wrong. Wrong!

CHRYSOTHEMIS: You could turn those words upon yourself.

ELECTRA: Ah, you don't think that I have said what is just.   1,040

CHRYSOTHEMIS: There are times when even justice can bring destruction.

49

ELECTRA: I could not live my life on such principles.

CHRYSOTHEMIS: If you make your attempt on Aegisthus
You will see that I am right.

ELECTRA: I will. You cannot frighten me.

CHRYSOTHEMIS: You will not change your mind? You're determined?

ELECTRA: The position you have taken makes you my enemy.

CHRYSOTHEMIS: So you will not listen to any of my advice?

ELECTRA: I am determined now. I was determined yesterday.

CHRYSOTHEMIS: Then I will leave you. You have no time
For my words, I none for your behavior.

ELECTRA: Yes, go. I will never call you back. Never—
Even if you longed for me to do so.
I am not a fool. It is over.

CHRYSOTHEMIS: You always think that only you are right.
Then think on! But when your troubles
Surround you, you will remember my words.

CHORUS: We see above us the birds
True to their nature,
For they care for those who gave them birth,
Those who gave them life.
Why can we not do the same?

Not long will they escape the thunderbolt of Zeus,
Not long Heaven's justice.
O Voice that goes to the dead,

50

Take a cry beneath the earth,
A cry that will scream its way
To the dead, the House of Atreus.
Tell them tales of woe locked in sorrow.

Tell them   1,070
That their house is sick,
That the two girls
Live in strife,
Live a life
Of discord and hate.
Electra,
Alone,
Betrayed,
Is wracked by grief.
Like the nightingale
She sings her grief,
Mourns her father
Ever in tears.
She has no thought of death,
Ready to leave the light
If she could rid the house
Of its two Furies.
Who was more nobly born?   1,080

The good will not live in shame,
If that means
Loss of name,
Loss of fame.
My child. My child.
You have chosen grief
And sorrow,
You have chosen honor
And the fame,
The double name
Of wise and brave,
Your father's child.

May you live a life
Of riches—
Your hand above
Your enemies
As you are now
Beneath their hand.
I have seen your anguish,
But I have seen the glory
Of your reverence of Zeus.

You understand the laws
Of God
Of Man.

ORESTES: (*disguised as a Phocian*)
Could you tell us please, ladies, if we have
Arrived at our destination—where we were
    directed?

CHORUS: What are you looking for? Why have you
come here?

ORESTES: I have been asking along the way for
Aegisthus' house.

CHORUS: This is his house. You were given the right
directions.

ORESTES: Could one of you tell those within of our
arrival?
It will be welcome news.

CHORUS: This lady here will give the message.

ORESTES: Could you tell them that some men from
Phocia
Are here to see Aegisthus?

ELECTRA: Oh god. Oh god! Before you came we
heard a rumor.
Do you bring proof, certain proof?

ORESTES: I know of no rumor. Old Strophius 1,110
Sent me with news of Orestes.

ELECTRA: Tell me. Tell me. I shudder with fear.

ORESTES: We have the little that is left of him
In this small urn, as you see.

ELECTRA: Oooh. (*weeps*) Here it is. It is finished.
My sorrow lies before my eyes.

ORESTES: If you are mourning for Orestes, for his
death,
This urn contains his body. This is now his
home.

ELECTRA: Sir, give it to me! By the Gods—if he
Is hidden in this urn—place him in my hands 1,120
That I may weep and grieve for all my race,
For myself and these his ashes.

ORESTES: (*to Pylades*)
Bring it here. Give it to her. Whoever she is,
She does not ask for it in hatred. She is
A friend perhaps, or one of his blood.

ELECTRA: Oh (*takes the urn*)
Is this all that is left of the soul of Orestes,
The man I loved most in the world? Is this
All that remains to remind me of him? I sent
you away in hope.
I receive you back again with none.
I hold in my hands nothingness. When I sent
you away
You gleamed in the light. Now nothingness. Oh
God. 1,130
How I wish you had left this life long ago
Before I sent you away to a strange country,
Before I stole you from them, with these two
hands

And saved you from death. If you had died
On that day you would have shared your
    father's grave,
Your right, your common due. Now far from
    home,
An exile, you died in a strange country.
Your death was painful and I was not there,
    your sister.
I did not, to my sorrow, wash your wounds.
These hands that loved you did not lift you up.
It was my right, my heavy grief, to lay you on
    the pyre   1,1
To burn in flames. But the hands of strangers
Gave you the last rites of death.
Now you come home to me,
A small weight in a small urn.
I mourn for you, mourn for the care I gave you
Long ago. I never left your side. The work was
    sweet
And all for nothing. I loved you.
I loved you more than your mother ever could.
I was your nurse. I was your family.
I can still hear you call me "sister, sister."
    Always.   1,1
Now all is gone. In one day you are dead.
Like a sudden storm you have destroyed
    everything
In the path of your departure from this life.
Our father is gone. I am dead in you. And you
    are dead.
And gone forever. Our enemies laugh.
Our mother, no mother, grows mad with joy.
You promised me so often, in secret messages,
That you would come to punish her.
But our God, yours and mine, this unlucky
    God,
Has taken this all away and sent you back to me

54

As dust and shadow instead of the shape I
  loved.
There is no help. Oh—Oh (*rhythmic wail*)   1,160
(*formal mourning*)

I mourn for your life.
Oh Oh.
You have gone on the saddest of journeys.
Oh Oh. My love. My brother.
You have ended my life, my brother.

Take me with you to the home of Death.
Nothing is nothing.
Let me live with you beneath the earth
Forever.
When you were on earth
We were one soul.
Now in death let me share
A grave with you.
The dead, I see, no longer suffer pain.   1,170

CHORUS: Remember, Electra, your father was
  mortal.
Orestes was mortal. Do not grieve too much.
Death is a debt that all of us must pay.

ORESTES: Ah.
What should I say? I am confused.
I have no control over what I want to say.

ELECTRA: What is the matter? What do you mean?

ORESTES: Are you Electra? the famous, the
  beautiful Electra?

ELECTRA: Yes, I am Electra, hardly the beautiful.

ORESTES: Oh God, the pain that you have suffered!

ELECTRA: Why do you pity me?   1,180

ORESTES: Cruel and inhuman torture.

55

ELECTRA: Yes, that has been my life.

ORESTES: A life without husband or happiness.

ELECTRA: Why do you look at me so? Why pity me?

ORESTES: My troubles were nothing. I knew nothing.

ELECTRA: What makes you say that?

ORESTES: I see how much you suffer.

ELECTRA: You see but a little of my pain.

ORESTES: How can there be more?

ELECTRA: I live with those that murdered him.   1,1

ORESTES: Who? Whose murderers?

ELECTRA: My father's. I am their slave. I have no choice.

ORESTES: Who forces you to be their slave?

ELECTRA: My—she is called my mother—but mother she is not.

ORESTES: How does she force you—violence or cruelty?

ELECTRA: Cruelty, violence, everything.

ORESTES: Do you have anyone to protect you or to stop her?

ELECTRA: No. There was. You have shown me his dust.

ORESTES: When I look at you I feel such sorrow, such grief.

ELECTRA: You are alone in your pity for me.   1,2

ORESTES: Yes. I came here alone. With you alone I shared your pain.

56

ELECTRA: Are you of our family, a blood relation?
Is that why you've come?

ORESTES: I will tell you. Is it safe to speak? (*of Chorus*)

ELECTRA: It is safe. They will say nothing.

ORESTES: Give me back the urn. I will tell you
everything.

ELECTRA: Don't take it from me. Please. I beg you.

ORESTES: It is for your own good. Do as I say.

ELECTRA: Do not take from me what I love most. I
beg you.

ORESTES: I cannot allow you to—

ELECTRA: Orestes! I cannot even bury you.   1,210

ORESTES: Careful of your words! They will bring
bad luck.
You have no right to mourn.

ELECTRA: No right to mourn for my dead brother?

ORESTES: Do not call him that.

ELECTRA: Am I so dishonored in my brother's eye?

ORESTES: No one dishonors you. You must not do
this.

ELECTRA: Yes, I grieve for Orestes here in my arms.

ORESTES: That is not him. That was a lie.

ELECTRA: Where is he buried then?

ORESTES: Nowhere. Only the dead are buried.

ELECTRA: What do you mean?

ORESTES: I tell the truth.   1,220

ELECTRA: Is he alive then?

57

ORESTES: Yes, if I am alive.

ELECTRA: You are he?

ORESTES: Look at this ring. It was our father's.
Do you believe me now?

ELECTRA: Most longed for day.

ORESTES: Most longed for, yes.

ELECTRA: That voice. Is it you?

ORESTES: Just listen. Just listen.

ELECTRA: Are you in my arms?

ORESTES: Forever.

ELECTRA: Dear, dear friends, women of the city.
Here is Orestes.
By trickery he died,
By trickery he lives safe in my arms. 1,2⁚

CHORUS: We see, my child. And your happiness
Makes us weep in happiness.

ELECTRA: Son of the man I loved best,
His son,
You have come at last,
You have come,
You have found us,
Known us whom you longed for.

ORESTES: Yes. I have come.
But you must wait and be silent.

ELECTRA: Why?

ORESTES: We must be silent so no one inside may
hear.

ELECTRA: I will never be afraid of her
No, by Artemis, eternal virgin goddess,

She, in there, is but a useless   1,240
Burden on the earth.

ORESTES: Remember that in women too
The spirit of war can breathe destruction.
You are living proof of that.

ELECTRA: Ah Ah Ah.
You have awakened my grief,
A grief as cruel as the sun,
That nothing can wash clean,
That cannot rest in oblivion,
That lives to haunt me.   1,250

ORESTES: I know. But you must wait to remember
    what was done.
Wait until your lips are free to speak.

ELECTRA: Every moment.
Every moment of my life is the right time to
    speak.

ORESTES: True. Then protect your freedom.

ELECTRA: How?

ORESTES: We have little time. Do not say too much.

ELECTRA: But you are with me.
How can I exchange silence   1,260
For the joy of seeing you.
Beyond hope,
Beyond all thought,
I see you again.

ORESTES: Yes. You see me now. The Gods told me it
    was time.

ELECTRA: Then you tell me words bathed
In even greater grace.
If the Gods sent you to this house
Your return is touched by divinity.   1,270

ORESTES: I do not want to curb your joy. And yet
   I fear that you will be overcome by happiness.

ELECTRA: Ah.
   You are here at last,
   At last you have made the journey
   That most I longed for.
   Do not now—
   Now that I see you
   After so much pain
   Do not—

ORESTES: Do not what?

ELECTRA: Deprive me of the joy of seeing your face.

ORESTES: No one can take me from you now.

ELECTRA: You promise?   1,2

ORESTES: Yes.

ELECTRA: My dearest Orestes; now I have heard the
      voice
   I dared not hope to hear again.
   I have restrained my passion in silence.
   I never screamed in pain when grief was upon
      me.
   But now I have you.
   I have your sweet face for my eyes to hold,
   The face that even in suffering I never forgot.

ORESTES: Now, tell me only what needs to be said.
   Do not tell me how evil my mother is.
   Nor how Aegisthus drains my father's wealth,   1,2
   Sucks it dry. To tell me this is to waste the time
   Of opportunity. Tell me what we need to know
   At this very moment. Should we hide or should
      we
   Move in the open and swiftly stop our enemies'
      laughter?

When we go inside you must be careful
That your mother does not see the radiance of
　your face.
She must not suspect. Weep for my death.
Mourn for me though I died in words alone.
When we have done what we must do
Then can you show your joy, then can you
　laugh,
Then can you be free.   1,300

ELECTRA: My brother, I am yours. This joy I feel
I got from you. It is not mine to own.
I would not hurt you for all the world.
To do so would be to hurt the god who now
Stands with us. You know what the situation is.
Aegisthus is not at home—as they told you—
Our mother is. Do not be afraid. She will not
　see
This face radiant with smiles. My hatred is too
　old   1,310
Too deep. Now that I have seen you I will weep,
Weep with joy. I cannot stop. For in one day
I have seen you dead and then alive.
What you have done for me is a miracle.
If my father were to come back to life and stand
Before me I would not wonder at it,
I would believe my eyes—as now I believe them.
You have come back to life and I will do
　whatever
You have in your heart. If I had been alone
I would have achieved one of two things,   1,320
A glorious life or a glorious death.

ORESTES: Quiet. I hear someone coming outside.

ELECTRA: (to Orestes and Pylades)
Go in, strangers and guests. Especially since
You bring what no one will refuse
Nor be happy when they receive it.

61

PAEDAGOGUS: Are you out of your minds? You
   fools!
  Have you no concern for your own lives?
  Have you no sense? Don't you see
  That you are not just near terrible danger
  But in its very midst? I have been standing
  By the door, waiting, watching, keeping guard.   1,3
  If I had not, your plans would now be in the
     house
  And long before you got there. I have been
  Your only protection. So stop all conversation
     now.
  Stop your unending cries of delight.
  Go in at once. If we delay any longer
  It will be disastrous. Now is the time to do it
     and be done.

ORESTES: When I go in what should I expect?

PAEDAGOGUS: It is good. No one could possibly
   recognize you.   1,3

ORESTES: You have announced my death.

PAEDAGOGUS: You have reached the House of
   Death—even as you live and breathe.

ORESTES: Were they happy with the news? What did
   they say?

PAEDAGOGUS: I will tell you when we are done. As
   it stands
  Everything is as they want and not as they
     expect.

ELECTRA: Brother, who is this man? Tell me.

ORESTES: You do not know him?

ELECTRA: I cannot even guess.

ORESTES: You do not know the man into whose
   hands you gave me?

ELECTRA: What, is this him?

ORESTES: In his hands and by your forethought   1,350
I was taken to Phocia.

ELECTRA: Is this him? He was the only one amongst
so many
Who stood by me when my father was
murdered.

ORESTES: This is the man. Question me no more.

ELECTRA: O most loved, O light most loved. You
alone
Have saved the House of Agamemnon.
Let me look at you. Was it you that saved
Orestes, saved me from our many sorrows?
O hands most loved,
Feet that saved our house from death.
How was it that when you came I stood beside
you
And I knew you not? You gave no hint. You
killed me
With your words but gave me back my life in joy.   1,360
Bless you, my father. I think I see my father.
Bless you, In one day I have hated you
Beyond hate and loved you beyond love.

PAEDAGOGUS: That is enough my child. There will
be time enough
In the days and nights to come to tell you,
Electra, of what has happened since I left.
(to Orestes and Pylades)
But now stand here no longer. It is time to act.
Clytemnestra is alone. No man is with her.
If you wait any longer you will have to fight   1,370
With others more cunning and more numerous
Than these.

ORESTES: Pylades, there is no time for words.
We must act. We must go within

63

And quickly. Only first a prayer
To the gods of my father's house,
The gods who live here before the palace.

ELECTRA: Apollo, hear their prayers.
Hear me too, lord. Often have I made you
    offerings.
Of the little I had I gave generously.
Apollo, lord, with all I have, I beg you,   1,3
Adore you, fall upon my knees,
Be kind to us. Bring our plans to success.
Show to all mankind the punishment
The Gods demand for evil and for sin.

CHORUS: See where the war god marches in
Breathing blood,
Breathing strife.
They have gone into the house.
Beneath the sheltering roof
The inescapable hounds of death
Are hunting,
Hunting the makers of evil.

Now the dream that hung in the air
Of my mind
Will pounce
And be done.

Into the house he goes,   1,3
The avenger of the dead,
Into his father's house.
Rich from of old he goes,
Stealth in the foot,
Stealth in the mind,
Blood in his hand,
Sharpened for Death.

Hermes, who brings the dead to darkness,
Brings the deed to darkness,

Brings it to its end
Now!

ELECTRA: Now is the moment, my friends,
When the men finish the deed.
Wait in silence.

CHORUS: What is happening?

ELECTRA: She is preparing the urn for burial. The
two of them   1,400
Are standing beside her.

CHORUS: Why are you out here?

ELECTRA: To watch for Aegisthus.
He must not come upon them unawares.

CLYTEMNESTRA: (*within*) Aagh.
House of Death. No friends. No friends.

ELECTRA: Did you hear the cry?

CHORUS: It struck terror in my soul.

CLYTEMNESTRA: Oh my God. Aegisthus, where are
you?

ELECTRA: Again she cries out.

CLYTEMNESTRA: My son, my son,   1,410
Pity your mother.

ELECTRA: You did not pity him
Nor the father who gave him life.

CHORUS: Oh my city, O cursed generations,
Now your unrelenting fate is dying, dying.

CLYTEMNESTRA: Aaa,
I am wounded.

ELECTRA: Strike again.

CLYTEMNESTRA: Again. I am struck again.

ELECTRA: If only Aegisthus were with you.

CHORUS: The curses end,
  The dead are alive.
  Men long dead are draining blood
  To answer blood   1,4
  From those that killed them.

  Here they come. Their hands are red with
    blood.
  They drip with the blood of sacrifice.
  There is no blame.

ELECTRA: Orestes, what has happened?

ORESTES: In the house, all is well
  If Apollo prophesied well.

ELECTRA: Is the wretched woman dead?

ORESTES: Lay your fears to rest.
  No more will your mother taunt you,
  No more dishonor you.

CHORUS: Stop, I can see Aegisthus coming.
  It is him.

ELECTRA: Go back to the house.   1,4

ORESTES: He is ours.

ELECTRA: Look how he smiles.
  Carefree he comes home.

CHORUS: Quick. Go back. Hide in the doorway.
  One is finished. Now the other.

ORESTES: Take heart. We will do it.

ELECTRA: Go then. Go where you wish.

ORESTES: I am gone.

ELECTRA: I will take care of things here.

66

CHORUS: Speak little. Speak gently.
Let him suspect nothing.   1,440
Let him go to do battle with Justice.

AEGISTHUS: Who knows where the Phocians are?
I've been told that they are here
And they have news of Orestes, that he
Lost his life in a chariot wreck.
You! Yes, you! I am talking to you.
You have opened your mouth enough times
    before.
This news is mainly your concern.
You should be able to tell me the truth.

ELECTRA: I know the truth. Yes. Otherwise I would
Be distant from what has happened to him I
    love best.

AEGISTHUS: Where are the strangers? Tell me.   1,450

ELECTRA: Inside. Their journey's end found a kind
    hostess.

AEGISTHUS: They report that his death is a fact?

ELECTRA: Not just a report—they have brought him
    with them.

AEGISTHUS: Can I see the body, here before my
    eyes?

ELECTRA: You can indeed. It is not a pretty sight.

AEGISTHUS: For once it is a pleasure to listen to you.
    Unusual.

ELECTRA: The pleasure is yours—if you can find it.

AEGISTHUS: That's enough. Open the doors. Let all
    Argos see.
Let Mycenae look upon this corpse,   1,460
And if any man holds empty hopes against me

67

Let him look and then accept my will.
Let him never think of meeting me with force,
For like this corpse he will regret it in death.

ELECTRA: My work is done. At last I have found
    sense.
And now I bow to those who wield the power.

AEGISTHUS: O Zeus. I look upon an image of one
    fallen
Not without the anger of the Gods. If that
Is blasphemy and brings the retribution of
    Nemesis,
I unsay it. Draw back the covering from the
    face.
Let me too mourn for one of my family's death.

ORESTES: Touch it yourself. This body does not
    belong to me.
It is yours alone. Look on it. Greet it with love.

AEGISTHUS: I will do as you say. It is good. You
    there,
Call Clytemnestra from the house.

ORESTES: She is near you. Look no further.

AEGISTHUS: Oh God, what is this?

ORESTES: Are you afraid? Do you know the face?

AEGISTHUS: Who are you?
Who are you that have cast this net of death
    around us?

ORESTES: You do not see that when you speak of the
    dead
You speak to the living?

AEGISTHUS: I understand. You are alive. You are
    Orestes.

68

ORESTES: The prophet speaks. Why so long in ignorance?

AEGISTHUS: This is my end then. One word! Let me say one—

ELECTRA: Not one. Not one word more. Brother, do not allow him to talk, I beg you.
Let him not linger and talk.
When a man is about to die time has no meaning.
Kill him quickly. When you have killed him,
Throw out the corpse to find suitable burial,
But out of our sight. This alone can pay me back
For all that I have suffered.   1,490

ORESTES: (*to Aegisthus*) Go inside and quickly. Words are not at stake.
Your life is.

AEGISTHUS: Why to the house? If what you do is good,
Why do you need the dark? Kill me here.

ORESTES: Give me no orders. Go inside. You will die
On the very spot where you murdered my father.

AEGISTHUS: Must necessity force this house to look upon
The present and the future evils of the house of Atreus?

ORESTES: Yours it shall look upon. Be sure of that.
In this I am an excellent prophet.

AEGISTHUS: Your father was no prophet.   1,500

ORESTES: Hold your tongue. It is time to go. Move.

AEGISTHUS: Lead the way.

ORESTES: No. You must go first.

AEGISTHUS: Afraid that I'll get away?

ORESTES: You will not choose how you will die.
I will make sure that you suffer a cruel death.
When men flaunt the law, justice will strike
them down,
Justice by death. Then there will be less men
like you.

CHORUS: O seed of Atreus, how much you have
suffered.
And how long—until you struggled to this
Moment of freedom. It is finished.   1,5

ELEPHANT PAPERBACKS

Literature and Letters
Stephen Vincent Benét, *John Brown's Body*, EL10
Isaiah Berlin, *The Hedgehog and the Fox*, EL21
Philip Callow, *Son and Lover: The Young D. H. Lawrence*, EL14
James Gould Cozzens, *Castaway*, EL6
James Gould Cozzens, *Men and Brethren*, EL3
Clarence Darrow, *Verdicts Out of Court*, EL2
Floyd Dell, *Intellectual Vagabondage*, EL13
Theodore Dreiser, *Best Short Stories*, EL1
Joseph Epstein, *Ambition*, EL7
André Gide, *Madeleine*, EL8
John Gross, *The Rise and Fall of the Man of Letters*, EL18
Irving Howe, *William Faulkner*, EL15
Aldous Huxley, *After Many a Summer Dies the Swan*, EL20
Aldous Huxley, *Ape and Essence*, EL19
Aldous Huxley, *Collected Short Stories*, EL17
Sinclair Lewis, *Selected Short Stories*, EL9
William L. O'Neill, ed., *Echoes of Revolt: The Masses,
    1911–1917*, EL5
Ramón J. Sender, *Seven Red Sundays*, EL11
Wilfrid Sheed, *Office Politics*, EL4
Tess Slesinger, *On Being Told That Her Second Husband Has
    Taken His First Lover, and Other Stories*, EL12
Thomas Wolfe, *The Hills Beyond*, EL16

Theatre and Drama
Robert Brustein, *Reimagining American Theatre*, EL410
Robert Brustein, *The Theatre of Revolt*, EL407
Irina and Igor Levin, *Working on the Play and the Role*, EL411
Plays for Performance:
    Aristophanes, *Lysistrata*, EL405
    Anton Chekhov, *The Seagull*, EL407
    Georges Feydeau, *Paradise Hotel*, EL403
    Henrik Ibsen, *Ghosts*, EL401
    Henrik Ibsen, *Hedda Gabler*, EL413
    Henrik Ibsen, *When We Dead Awaken*, EL408
    Heinrich von Kleist, *The Prince of Homburg*, EL402
    Christopher Marlowe, *Doctor Faustus*, EL404
    The Mysteries: Creation, EL412
    The Mysteries: The Passion, EL414
    Sophocles, *Electra*, EL415
    August Strindberg, *The Father*, EL406

ELEPHANT PAPERBACKS

American History and American Studies
Stephen Vincent Benét, *John Brown's Body*, EL10
Henry W. Berger, ed., *A William Appleman Williams Reader*,
    EL126
Andrew Bergman, *We're in the Money*, EL124
Paul Boyer, ed., *Reagan as President*, EL117
Robert V. Bruce, *1877: Year of Violence*, EL102
George Dangerfield, *The Era of Good Feelings*, EL110
Clarence Darrow, *Verdicts Out of Court*, EL2
Floyd Dell, *Intellectual Vagabondage*, EL13
Elisha P. Douglass, *Rebels and Democrats*, EL108
Theodore Draper, *The Roots of American Communism*, EL105
Joseph Epstein, *Ambition*, EL7
Paul W. Glad, *McKinley, Bryan, and the People*, EL119
Daniel Horowitz, *The Morality of Spending*, EL122
Kenneth T. Jackson, *The Ku Klux Klan in the City, 1915–1930*,
    EL123
Edward Chase Kirkland, *Dream and Thought in the Business
    Community, 1860–1900*, EL114
Herbert S Klein, *Slavery in the Americas*, EL103
Aileen S. Kraditor, *Means and Ends in American Abolitionism*,
    EL111
Leonard W. Levy, *Jefferson and Civil Liberties: The Darker Side*,
    EL107
Seymour J. Mandelbaum, *Boss Tweed's New York*, EL112
Thomas J. McCormick, *China Market*, EL115
Walter Millis, *The Martial Spirit*, EL104
Nicolaus Mills, ed., *Culture in an Age of Money*, EL302
Roderick Nash, *The Nervous Generation*, EL113
William L. O'Neill, ed., *Echoes of Revolt: The Masses,
    1911–1917*, EL5
Glenn Porter and Harold C. Livesay, *Merchants and
    Manufacturers*, EL106
Edward Reynolds, *Stand the Storm*, EL128
Geoffrey S. Smith, *To Save a Nation*, EL125
Bernard Sternsher, ed., *Hitting Home: The Great Depression in
    Town and Country*, EL109
Athan Theoharis, *From the Secret Files of J. Edgar Hoover*, EL127
Nicholas von Hoffman, *We Are the People Our Parents Warned
    Us Against*, EL301
Norman Ware, *The Industrial Worker, 1840–1860*, EL116
Tom Wicker, *JFK and LBJ: The Influence of Personality upon
    Politics*, EL120
Robert H. Wiebe, *Businessmen and Reform*, EL101
T. Harry Williams, *McClellan, Sherman and Grant*, EL121
Miles Wolff, *Lunch at the 5 & 10*, EL118